12-25-2017

Dear Sarah, Scott,
    Will & Joey

    This Christian reading is a one of a kind!

    The author, an incredible woman, has learned the magic way to reach children with Christianity.

    If you enjoy, and would like another, please let me know. I have been blest to meet and friends with the author now.

            Happy Reading
        & God bless —
                Aunt Sharon

Hi!
We are the real
Stufffeds!

Duffy

Tudious Foo

Sliver

Snooper

Annabelle

SLIVER'S HATS

God is
faithful and just.

1 John 1:8-9

Written and Illustrated

by

Denice Goldschmidt

1

Many Thanks!

Many people have blessed me with their expertise
and given me support as I produced this book.

To **Victor,** my husband: Your patience, your daily support and your keen eye for design, has been helpful beyond measure. I thank you!

To **Lisa Feringa**: Thank you for the accountability, encouragement and prayer we've shared during our biweekly meetings.   You are a faithful writing partner!

To my daughters, **Lisa Marion Spangenberg** and **Leanna Bolden**, and to **Carolyn Moses**, my prayer partner of many years: How I thank each of you for the hours of editing you gave!

To **Patti Peterson**: Sliver and I thank you for the inspiration for her favorite hat!

To **Sylvia**, the real Sliver, wherever you are: I fondly remember our time together in our college freshman dorm.* I am honored to have you as Annabelle's best friend.

To my **Prayer Team**: I could not have done this book without your prayer support. My deep felt thanks to each one of you!

And best of all, to my **Heavenly Father**: You called me to this work. I thank You and I humbly give You all the glory.

Text and Illustrations Copyright © 2013 by Denice Goldschmidt
Published by Art Images, P.O. Box 423, Northport, MI 49670-0423
Printed in the U.S.A. by Village Press, Traverse City, MI 49686

Scripture quotations are taken from the Holy Bible, New International Version, Copyright © 1985 by the Zondervan Corporation.

*Haven Hall, Syracuse University, Syracuse, New York, 1954

ISBN 978-0-615-77541-8

I dedicate this book to my very dear friend,

Carolyn J. Moses.

Carolyn,
the Lord Jesus has blessed our friendship for more than 40 years!
Even now as we continue as long distance prayer partners,
we are close because He is our center!

Indeed,

Our times together are so rich!

Meet the Stufffeds!

Hi! I'm Miss Prissy, first on the left, above. I like to cook for all of us, and of course, to be a part of the up *and* down times we share together. We are stuffed. That's why we're called the Stufffeds (*pronounced Stuff-eds*).

Duffy, the round, fat bear above, is very furry and soft. He eats moonbeams, which make him very light. He has a hard time keeping on the ground. When he walks, he bounces!

Snooper is our delightful puppy dog. Even though he sometimes gets into trouble, his heart is full of love. He has colorful patches that hold him together and keep him from losing his stuffing.

Annabelle is a stuffed doll like I am. I have fun braiding her long, red braids. I like watching them flop when she runs. Snooper is special to Annabelle. When he gets into trouble, she's always right there to help him.

Now you have met the Stufffeds! Come join us in the story that follows. We want you to meet Sliver, Annabelle's wild and fun friend.

On The Way to Their Picnic

"Why is the highest sand dune the one between our homes?" asked Annabelle, digging her feet in the sand as she climbed.

"Maybe it's a test of our friendship," Sliver declared.

"Nothing will ever break that!" Annabelle vowed as they pulled each other to the top.

"What a beautiful day!" Annabelle exclaimed, as she plopped down to rest. "And not a cloud in the sky! Perfect day for our picnic."

"Sure is," Sliver agreed, catching her breath. "Is everyone coming?"

"Yup," Annabelle answered.

"That means Snooper-dawg is coming. Why do you even like him?"

"He's my watch dog!" Annabelle said. "Well, most of the time I'm *his* watch dog!" she added, laughing.

"He's such a pest," Sliver claimed. "Not like Duffy."

"How's that?" Annabelle asked.

"Duffy minds his own business. Snooper, though, always wants to try on my hats."

"So? Why not let him?"

"No way!" Sliver insisted, lifting her nose. "He'll *never* get to."

Annabelle ignored Sliver's comment. "I love the hat you lent me today," she said. Hopping to her feet, she twirled in the warm sunshine. Braids and ribbons trailed in tandem.

"You're my best friend, Annabelle. You get to try on *all* the hats I make!" Sliver gave Annabelle a big hug. "Hey!" she added. "I'll race you down the dune to the beach!"

Off the girls dashed through swirling sand. "Wow! Whoa!" Annabelle yelled as she tripped, tumbled and slid her way down.

"Ouch!" she exclaimed, landing with a thud. "I'm glad I wasn't carrying the cookies we just made! They'd be crumbs!" After brushing off sand, she reached for her hat in the dune grass and straightened her crunched backpack.

"Speaking of cookies," Sliver said with a sly glint in her eye. "Let's snitch one. I'm starved!" She reached for a cookie from her bag.

"No!" Annabelle insisted. "We want to be sure we have enough for everyone."

"Oh, okay," Sliver agreed. "Hey, I brought ribbons," she added. "Will you braid my hair at the picnic? This time I want long fronds."

"Sliver, one of your fun words again! What are fronds?"

"These!" Sliver said as she flipped the fringes of Annabelle's red braids. "Well, I sort of made it up. But it fits. Fronds are the leaves on ferns. Long and floppy. That's how I want the ends of my braids."

"Long, floppy fronds you will have," Annabelle announced with a giggle.

"I'm glad Miss Prissy is coming to the picnic," Sliver said. "I always have fun with her when I'm at your house. I think she likes me."

"I know she does," Annabelle assured her.

"I like her funny shoes!" Sliver exclaimed. "Ooooh, I'd love to try them on!"

"You're silly, Sliver. But that's what I like about you," Annabelle said as they skipped along the beach to meet the others.

The Picnic

Snooper watched Annabelle and Sliver run along the beach. *Why does Annabelle have to bring her?* he thought. *And – yup, they both have new hats.*

"Here they come!" Duffy yelled, bouncing with delight.

"Miss Prissy!" Sliver said, breathless. "We brought the cookies. And we made them just like you showed us!"

"Mmm, they smell good!" Miss Prissy exclaimed, placing them in the picnic basket.

As they all took the path through the woods to the pond, Snooper sided up to Annabelle. "Hey," he whispered, "may I try on your hat?"

Before Annabelle could respond, Sliver jumped between them. "No!" she declared. "That's *my* hat and you may *not* try it on!"

Snooper backed away and lagged behind.
Why won't she ever let me try on her hats? he thought, hanging his head.

"When we get to our picnic spot, I'm going to fish," Duffy announced. His pole bobbed on his furry shoulder.

"We brought books," Annabelle said. "And I'm also going to braid Sliver's hair."

"I have my Bible and journal," Miss Prissy chimed in, patting her skirt pocket.

Snooper's head popped up. "I'm going to sniff under rocks. I hope I find lots of bugs."

"UGH!" Sliver yelled. She scooted away from Snooper. "Bugs! Just stay away from me!"

When they reached their picnic spot, warm sunlight filtered through the trees.
Sparkles danced on the pond's bright blue reflection of the sky.
There was no breeze, just birds chirping their glad welcome.

"Annabelle and Duffy, will you please help me hang the hammock?" Miss Prissy asked.

"I'll spread the blanket and set out the lunch," Sliver announced. She placed her hat on the blanket, reserving a spot for herself in the sun.

Wow – that hat would look so good on me, Snooper thought. "Hey, Sliver, may I try on your hat, just once? Pleeease?" he begged.

Sliver simply glared at him.

"Guess not," he mumbled, slinking from her view.

It didn't take long for their lunch of sandwiches, fruit and fresh vegetables to disappear. After enjoying the freshly baked cookies, they decided Miss Prissy would have the hammock first. Duffy baited his fishing hook, and Snooper ventured into the woods to scamper and sniff.

"Sliver, let's go sit under those trees," Annabelle suggested.

"Yeah! We want to be by ourselves," Sliver said, arm in arm with Annabelle.

They settled at the base of a towering oak tree. "Oh, this is so peaceful," Sliver sighed, fingering the fallen acorns. "Watch Duffy," she whispered.

As he cast his fishing line again and again, it skimmed the surface of the glimmering pond.

"And look at Miss Prissy," Sliver added. "I think she's falling asleep."

Annabelle yawned. "I'd better braid your hair soon before *I* fall asleep!"

While Annabelle twisted Sliver's fluffy hair, Sliver shifted about, trying to get comfortable.

"Why are you wiggling, Sliver? Please hold still. I'm almost done."

"I itch," Sliver complained, scratching her legs through her jeans. "And my back itches," she added, twisting and squirming.

Suddenly, "ARGH!" she shrieked. "HELP! HELP!"

She jumped up. Her arms thrashed and slapped at her legs and back.

"BUGS!" she screamed at the top of her lungs. "BUGS!"

Duffy looked over from his fishing. *Bugs? They make good bait,* he thought.

Miss Prissy's eyes popped open. She rolled off the hammock and rushed to the commotion. She brushed Sliver's pant legs as Annabelle swept bugs from Sliver's shirt.

14

Snooper also heard the uproar. He raced from the woods and slid to a halt. "I can shake your hat and things," he offered.

"NO!" Sliver screamed. "It's all your fault! You and your bugs!"

"But...but, I didn't..." stammered Snooper.

"Oh, dear," Miss Prissy murmured, noting Sliver's anger.

When Sliver calmed down, Miss Prissy suggested they all call it a day. The sun had slipped low and long shadows brought a late afternoon chill. It was time to go home.

"You three go ahead," Miss Prissy said after everything was gathered. "Sliver and I will fold the hammock and be right along."

New Life

The others had gone ahead, leaving Sliver and Miss Prissy to follow.

"They're way ahead of us," Sliver complained as they padded along. "And I can't carry this heavy hammock!"

Suddenly, Sliver stumbled and sent the hammock flying.

Her hat popped from her head and slid in the grass. "*I* will get it," she snipped. After grabbing her hat, she examined it and held it close.

"I knew I shouldn't have come," she grumbled, near tears. "And that – that hammock – is too big a load for me to carry."

16

"My, my…" mused Miss Prissy. She set the lunch basket down and sat near Sliver. "Yes, you are carrying quite a load."

"Call one of the others – Snooper – he deserves to carry it," Sliver said, pouting.

"I was thinking of another load you're carrying, Sliver."

"Huh?" Sliver looked around.

"It's the anger you have toward Snooper."

"I'm not angry," she snapped. "Well, maybe I am, sort of. He always wants to try on my hats. He just gets in the way."

"You're using your hats, Sliver – as lovely as they are – to cover something deep in your heart. Tell me how Snooper gets in the way."

"I don't see why Annabelle likes him so much."

"Are you afraid she won't like you if she likes him?"

Sliver slumped and stared at the ground. "I guess so," she sighed, the truth pouring out.

Miss Prissy looked at Sliver. She could see her pain. "Sliver, do you think you might be jealous?"

Sliver cocked her head to one side. Before she could say a word, Miss Prissy continued. "Jealousy is a sin, Sliver, and it can lead to anger and hate and lost friendships."

"I don't want that," Sliver said. "I want Annabelle to like me."

"Oh, Sliver, she likes you very much. But it's time to deal with this sin of jealousy that keeps you stuck in unkind behavior."

"Didn't Jesus die on the cross for my sin?" Sliver asked. "So – how has this happened to me?"

"Jesus did die on the cross for your sin," Miss Prissy responded. "But sometimes – like what's happened to you – we get so caught in a sin, we can't see our way out."

Sliver sighed. "I know I've been awful, and yes, I'm – I'm jealous. I've tried to stop being mean, but I can't do anything about it."

"You can't on your own," Miss Prissy explained, "but God has given us a doorway to freedom from the power of sin."

She pulled her Bible from her skirt pocket. Sliver slid beside her and watched as she carefully turned the well-worn pages to 1 John 1:8-9.

"Listen to these verses," Miss Prissy said.

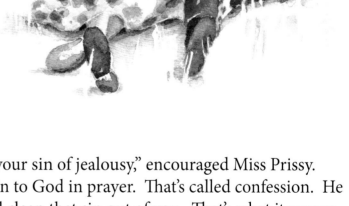

"If we claim to be without sin, we deceive ourselves and the truth is not in us. If we confess our sins, He is faithful and just and will forgive us our sins and purify us from all unrighteousness."

"Sliver, You've been honest about your sin of jealousy," encouraged Miss Prissy. "The next thing is to admit your sin to God in prayer. That's called confession. He will forgive you, Sliver, and He will clean that sin out of you. That's what it means when He says He purifies us from all unrighteousness."

Sliver stared ahead. Miss Prissy sat still and waited.

"But, Miss Prissy, what happens if it doesn't work?"

"God will do His part, just as He says. He also wants *you* to do *your* part."

"You mean I have to *do* something?"

Sliver flopped on her back. "I thought those verses say that God does it all."

"We become a partner with God," Miss Prissy explained. "Your part is to believe Him and to repent. That means you make an effort to change the way you think and act."

"Help," Sliver moaned. "It's too much for me!"

"I can't do it either, Sliver – not alone. I call upon Jesus to help when I'm stuck in sin. He sends His Holy Spirit to comfort and guide me. He makes it easier."

Sliver lay very still, thinking. Suddenly – up she sat.

"Miss Prissy, I want to stop being so mean! Will you help me pray?"

Sliver began to pray, admitting her sin of jealousy. Miss Prissy encouraged her to tell God her fear of losing Annabelle's friendship – and to acknowledge how awful she'd been to Snooper.

"And God, I *really* want You to forgive me. Please clean me of all un – unrighteousness, like Your Word says. I want my heart right. And will Your Holy Spirit *please* help me to change the way I think and act? I don't want to be mean anymore. Thank You! Amen."

Sliver was quiet as she chewed her braid.

"Miss Prissy," she said with caution, "can Annabelle like both Snooper and me?"

"Oh, yes. That's what God's love is like – more than enough for everyone."

"Can I still make my hats?"
Sliver's eyes were filled with worry.

"Yes, yes," Miss Prissy answered with a chuckle.

"Miss Prissy, do I have to let Snooper try on, you know, my best hats?"

"No."

"Can I decide which ones?"

"Yes. Yes, you can, Sliver."

Sliver hopped to her feet.
"I know what I'm going to do, Miss Prissy! It's going to be a big surprise! You'll see!"

"Oh! Everything is lighter," she added, swinging the hammock over her shoulder. "Miss Prissy, thank you for showing me how to get rid of the *real* load I was carrying!"

The Big Surprise

"I do *not* want to go!"

Snooper kicked the sand and lagged behind Duffy and Annabelle as they climbed the dune to Sliver's house. She had invited them to lunch, and her invitation said it was a "Big Surprise Party."

"She didn't mean to invite me," Snooper grumbled. "She doesn't even like me."

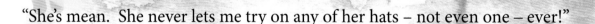

"Snooper, let's stop for a minute," Annabelle said. She sat on the sand facing Snooper.

Duffy wiggled a hollow spot in the sand and nestled in. He knew this would take some time.

"Snooper – is it really that *you* don't like *her*?" Annabelle asked.

"She's mean. She never lets me try on any of her hats – not even one – ever!"

"I know that, Snooper, and it makes me sad."

"Not one," Snooper repeated, stamping his paw.

"Snooper, you can't change her, but you can –"

"I know, I know," Snooper interrupted. "I know what you're going to say."

"My favorite verses," Duffy anticipated, clapping his paws.

"And I know them," Snooper sighed, "I have to confess my part – my sin." Without any urging, his eyes slipped closed as he sank down in the sand.

"Jesus, I really, *really* want to try on one of Sliver's handmade hats. I confess I've been angry with her, and selfish, too, thinking only about myself. Please forgive me and help me to accept her the way she is. And will You help me – *try* – to enjoy her party? Amen."

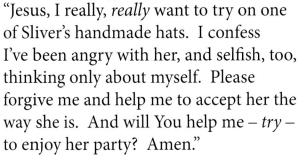

"Good going, Snooper," Annabelle declared, giving him a friendly nudge.

"Changing my attitude – that will be the hard part," Snooper added with a sigh.

Duffy jumped up.

"God is faithful and just," he announced, "and He will forgive you of your sin and will purify you of all unrighteousness!"

"I know, I know, Duffy," Snooper agreed, still not sure he could trust Jesus to do it.

When they arrived at Sliver's house, the front door was wide open. "Yoo-hoo!" Annabelle called. "Anyone home?"

"I'll get it," a familiar voice responded.

"Miss Prissy!" Duffy declared. "When did you get here?"

"A few minutes ago," Miss Prissy said, welcoming them in. "Sliver wants us to wait here in the entryway – part of her surprise."

Snooper was the first to see Sliver as she swept down the stairs to greet her guests.

Another new hat, he noticed.

Remembering his prayer, he chose to think of the yummy lunch smells instead of Sliver and her hats.

"Hi, everyone!" Sliver exclaimed. "This is great! All of you made it. First, everyone has to wear a blindfold," she instructed.

"Miss Prissy is going to lead you upstairs to the playroom. Something special is waiting for us there."

Wearing their blindfolds, they carefully climbed the steps and waited for Sliver's directions.

"Miss Prissy," Sliver whispered, "how does everything look?"

"Beautiful," she replied, giving a thumbs-up.

"Okay," Sliver announced. "You may take off your blindfolds!"

Off flew Annabelle's and Duffy's. Snooper slowly removed his, not sure he wanted to see.

"Sliver!" Annabelle exclaimed, staring around the room.

Duffy bounced high with glee. "Whee – eeee!"

The whole room was tastefully decorated with hat after hat after hat. Hats were on stands and on the table. Hats hung on the wall. Hats swung from the backs of chairs. Hats clung to a hat tree.

"I have a surprise," Sliver said, reaching for a hat. "I made this one for someone very special." As she caressed the hat, she walked straight to Snooper and placed it on his head. Snooper stood there frozen.

26

"Come, Snooper – look in the mirror!" Sliver said excitedly.

Oh, he thought. *Oh! I love it!*
"How – how long may I wear it?"

"Forever, Snooper. I made it for you. It's yours!"

Snooper kept staring, first in the mirror, then at Sliver. "Sliver, I – I love it," he stammered. He looked again in the mirror, following his image as he turned his head. "It's so handsome! Thank you! Thank you!"

"Snooper – this is very important," Sliver said. "See those bugs decorating your hat? I have an urgent – no, a desperate request – that they stay right there on your hat!" Everyone laughed as they gathered to admire the tiny, handmade bugs.

"And now," Sliver announced, "everyone can pick a hat to wear to lunch."

Hmmm, Snooper thought as he looked at all the hats in the room. *Wow! There are so many!* "But this one? It's the best!" he exclaimed, patting his own. With a swing in his step and his head held high, he joined the hat parade to lunch.

From Sliver's Journal

The day after my Hat Party:

My Surprise Hat Party turned out just like I wanted! Everyone loved the new hats I made. It was fun to watch Snooper during lunch. He kept adjusting his hat and he excused himself twice to look in the mirror!

I love the hats everyone chose to wear to lunch. We took photos of each one of us.   Here they are!

Snooper
in his hat!
Handsome Bug Boy!

Perfect for Miss P!
She helped me
knit this one!
She is _so_ cool!

Dapper Duff!
I knew Duffy would
choose this one!

I _love_ Annabelle's choice. I made this hat with her in mind. She asked me to fix her braids like mine!

Oh!
This is my
favorite
hat!

After lunch, Snooper and I talked. I told him how jealous I had been. I am very thankful he forgave me for being so mean. He shared how angry he was and how he confessed his selfishness to Jesus. We are amazed at how God's words in 1 John 1:8-9 helped us both!

I am memorizing those verses!
(I wear a hat so they won't leak out of my head!)

"If we claim to be without sin, we deceive ourselves (Oh! I don't want to do that!) and the truth is not in us. If we confess our sins, He (God) is faithful and just and will forgive us our sins (Wow, I am so thankful!) and purify us from all unrighteousness." (That means, He makes us right again!).

Annabelle is still my very best friend,
but now I know we both can have lots of friends
and not lose what's special between us.

Our friendship is like God's love; lots to spread around!

The best hat I ever made was Snooper's.
I giggle when he tries on other ones.
He always says,
"Oh, I look soooo good in this hat!"

Hmmmm.
Whose hat will I make next?

THE END

From the Heart of Miss Prissy

When I discovered 1 John 1:8-9 in the Bible,
I decided to take God at His Word and do exactly as He says.
As soon as I confess a sin to Him, He lifts it from me.
He gives me the strength to change my attitude and actions,
just like He did for Sliver.

We all sin. It's something we do or think that does not please God.
He tells us what those things are in His Word, the Bible.
When you sin, don't run *from* God...run *to* Him!

Confess it out loud to Jesus like Snooper did.
As your Savior and Friend, He will forgive you and free you from your sin.
Then His Holy Spirit will bless you with His peace and joy!

Oh! I pray you will choose this freedom God offers you!

Love from,

Miss Prissy ☺